Serafina's Wish

Written By Eleanor Moseley Pollnow
Illustrated By Nicole Stremlow Monahan

Serafina's Wish

For Nor and Ben, with love.

2017

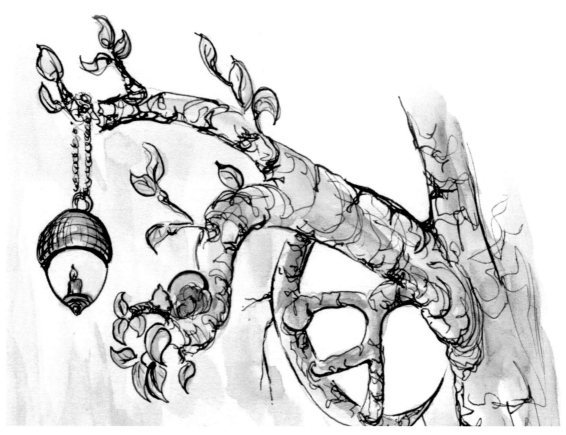

Serafina's family had always lived in treehouses, high up in the old oaks overlooking the village. Warmed by the sun and washed clean by the rain, their cozy homes swayed in the breeze. Squirrels chattered in the windows and hummingbirds sometimes hid their tiny nests in the walls.

Before Serafina was born, her Mama and Papa had waited and hoped and wished for a baby. When Serafina finally arrived, pink and strong and very, very loud, they had a celebration. Mama and Papa and her grandparents all crowded around her bassinet as it rocked from the branches of the ceiling.

Her aunts and uncles and cousins all joined in from the neighboring trees to sing "Welcome to the Wonderful World, Little One" in three-part harmony.

Serafina grew, curly-haired and fearless. She scampered like a monkey up the branches and across the swaying bridges that connected one family tree to the next.

When she was old enough for school in the Down-Below, she climbed down to join the village children. Serafina loved going to school, loved the painting and the dancing and the ukulele sing-alongs, but she was always happy to climb back up to their treehouse in the sky and be with her Mama and Papa.

Coming home from school one day, she surprised a squirrel at her pillow.

He jumped to the windowsill and froze, looking at her.

Serafina lifted the pillow to find a single perfect acorn, bigger than any she had ever seen, dark and shiny smooth. "Is this a special acorn?" Serafina asked the squirrel. He flicked his tail twice and leapt out of sight. Carefully, Serafina tucked the acorn back away. "Yes. I think it is."

Just as her parents had hoped and wished for her, Serafina hoped and wished for a little brother or sister. Month after month, she fell asleep with her special acorn in her hand, wishing for a baby.

Soon, little Button was born, and she joined the family chorus singing in harmony around his little bassinet.

"Thank you, Acorn!" Serafina smiled to herself.

Button was a fine fellow, waving his chubby fists with delight when Serafina danced and sang and juggled eggs for him. She helped him grow his teeth by rubbing on his gums. She taught him how to climb, little branches at first, then bigger ones, and she taught him to hold on tight and cross the treebridges safely.

Button loved his big sister as much as he loved the sunshine and the sound of birdsong, and he grew bigger and bigger every day.

Living so close to the sky, Serafina had one secret, impossible wish. She dreamed of a horse with great wings that she could ride up into the wide, wild blue.

Every year as she blew out the candles on her birthday cake, she wished for "a flying horse, a flying horse, a flying horse!" But birthdays brought books and sweaters and cakes. Still, as she fell asleep on her birthday eve, Serafina would clutch her special acorn and fiercely make the same wish.

"It never hurts to dream!" she told herself.

As she and Button grew, their tiny treehouse became more and more crowded. Button's bed bumped against hers, his toys jumbled into her collection of treasures, and he growled and snorted in his sleep like a loud little bear cub.

When Serafina grumped at breakfast about being woken in the night, Papa said, "Oh, now, Button doesn't know any better." "Yes," smiled Mama, "he's a noisy sleeper. Just like his Papa."

Hummph, grumbled Serafina.

The night before Serafina's twelfth birthday, Papa made the children promise not to peek out the window all night. Button snored peacefully, but Serafina lay listening and wondering as Mama and Papa and her aunts and uncles and the older cousins worked into the night. At long last she slept, and at sunrise Serafina emerged to find everyone waiting to show her the great surprise.

A new treehouse had been built in the night, its leafy roof rustling in the morning breeze: a treehouse just for her, at the tip-top of their family tree. Serafina scampered up and pushed open the door. It was perfect, with a nook by the window waiting for her bed, an empty bookshelf waiting for all her treasures, and best of all, a large door opening onto a broad wooden deck.

Serafina stepped outside, spread her
arms wide and laughed out loud.

She felt like the captain of a great ship, riding a green sea of leaves under the wide, wild blue sky. It was almost as good as flying. "Thank you, oh thank you! Thank you! Thank you!!!!" She warbled, and her voice carried across all the trees. From all the neighboring oaks, voices called back "You're welcome! You're welcome! You're welcome!"

Mama and Papa came beaming out onto the deck, and Button joined her at the railing, looking out at the world below. "Can I can come up and play?" he asked longingly. "Yes!" laughed his sister, giving his hand a squeeze "and maybe someday I'll invite you over for a sleepover."

I never wished for this, but Oh! this makes me happy, Serafina smiled to herself. I guess life can bring you impossible surprises. Sometimes they're just different from what you thought you were wishing for.

Eleanor Moseley Pollnow is an actor, playwright, mother, and grandmother. She and her husband Charlie live in a house firmly planted on the ground.

Nicole Stremlow Monahan is an illustrator and art instructor, whose studio is tucked away in the wild and ferny woods outside of Seattle.

Made in the USA
San Bernardino, CA
21 December 2017